P9-DEF-905

LITTLE MAVERICK COW

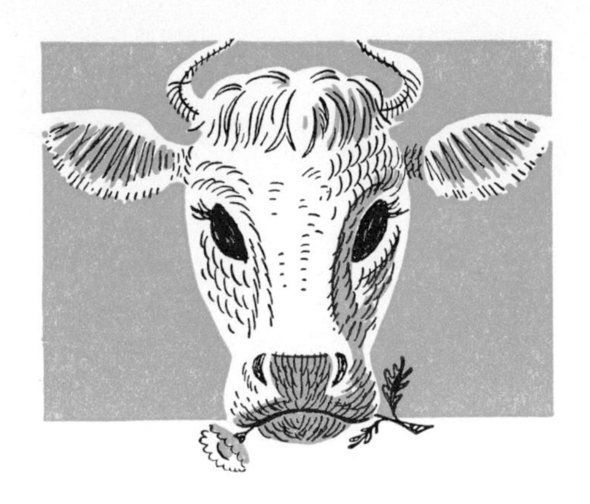

LITTLE MAVERICK COW

by

BELLE COATES

Illustrated by George Fulton

CHARLES SCRIBNER'S SONS New York

Printed in the United States of America A-10.56 [J]

LIBRARY OF CONGRESS CATALOG CARD NUMBER 57–5167

To my mother

LITTLE MAVERICK COW

CHAPTER I

Breakfast was over at Knoll Ranch in Montana. Sue and Todd were ready in their jeans and cowboy boots to help Mother and Dad plan the day's work.

Dad began gently with some bad news. "Our cow died last night."

For a moment Sue and Todd couldn't speak. They looked out of the kitchen window at their sparkling white hens in the dooryard.

They looked at their roan pony, Calico, dozing in the corral.

They looked at their great oblong of wheat on the slope, turning from green to brown in the dry Montana sunshine.

They looked, but all they saw was *no more cow!*

"If old Brindle is dead," said Todd finally, "we'll just have to buy us another cow."

Dad believed in facing things when you are seven and eight. He said, "We've just bought us a little wheat ranch. We have no money to buy another cow. Not until the wheat crop is in next fall."

"Jody needs milk *now,*" said Sue, with an anxious glance at the baby kicking in his crib.

"You and Todd need milk, too," said Mother, beginning to clear the table.

It was very bad to lose their only milch cow.

"What shall we *do* about it, Dad?" asked Todd.

"The first thing to do," said Dad, smiling into Todd's earnest eyes, "is to help Mother make Jody's formula of canned milk, so he may have some breakfast, too. After that we will decide what next."

When Dad smiled like that Sue and Todd always knew there was a way out of their trouble.

Todd squared his shoulders. "I'll feed the chickens while you help Mother," he said to Sue.

"When our work is done may we ride up the knoll to the Lookout Seat and watch the Rocking A cattle?" asked Sue.

Mother and Dad were willing. An hour later Todd took the pair of old field glasses from their hook and slung the strap over his shoulder. Sue made peanut butter sandwiches. Then they saddled Calico and rode her double up the steep knoll trail that led to the Lookout Seat.

"Maybe," said Todd in the saddle, "we can think of a way to get us a cow."

Behind him Sue sighed. "We can't get us a cow by looking at our neighbor's cows."

"Anyway, it's fun to look," said Todd. "I like *all* cows. And I like our new wheat ranch. I want to stay here always, don't you, Sue?"

CHAPTER II

At the top of the knoll there was a pile of rocks, jumbled together like giant ABC blocks. Some of them spilled through the barbed wires of the Rocking A fence that stretched out of sight on both sides. On the top of the pile there was one rock that was shaped like a big armchair. Sue and Todd called it the Lookout Seat.

They tied Calico to a scrub chokecherry tree and climbed over the rocks to the Lookout Seat. It was warmed by the sun and serene and above everything else. They could see for miles around.

There were the high plains of Montana with hundreds of white-faced beef cattle grazing upon them. These cattle belonged to the Rocking A Ranch.

"You take first turn with the field glasses," said Todd. "Let's see what's going on in the herd today."

From the Lookout Seat life on the plains was new and real and exciting. The field glasses brought the far-away close up. "Like the opera," said Sue, remembering the one they saw with Aunt Matilda last winter.

Todd didn't feel like the opera today. He

felt down to earth. He looked across the barbed wire fence at the hundreds of Rocking A cattle. He thought of old Brindle and their empty cow barn.

"I wish *we* had just one of those cows," he said.

"Those are beef cattle out there, not milch cows," said Sue. "Red and Lowly told us there's a difference."

Red and Lowly were the Rocking A cowboys who rode fence and tended the herd. Sometimes they stopped below the Lookout Seat to visit across the fence with Sue and Todd. They knew all about cattle.

"I know there's a difference between milch cows and beef cows," said Todd. "Lowly said that beef cows don't give enough milk to make them worth milking. But Lowly winked when he said that."

Sue laughed as she adjusted the field glasses. "Red and Lowly say sober things with funny faces, and funny things with sober faces. We never know if they *mean* what they say."

Todd grinned. "I wish they'd ride by today."

Sue began to look at the great beef herd through the field glasses. Their sameness charmed her. All of them had white faces bent to the grass. All had red sides with white trim along their backs or under their middles. All of them wore the Rocking A brand proudly, like a badge, on their left shoulders.

"There's a new calf over on the ridge," said Sue. "He's just learning to stand up! Look at him."

She gave Todd a look. Through the glasses Todd saw the little white-faced calf rock back and forth, then lunge to his feet. His legs got tangled. He fell back on the grass.

"He won't make it until he learns to use his hind legs first," said Todd.

"He made it!" said Sue finally, when it was her turn to look. "His mother helped him with a little bunt."

In a few minutes Todd said, "They're all starting down to drink over on the west slope. It must be nearly noon. Let's eat our sandwiches."

The range cattle started to drink at the same time each day, as if they went by a clock in the sky. Sue and Todd ate their sandwiches and watched the cattle move slowly, like a string of red ants, down the cowpath to the water hole.

"Here come Red and Lowly!" said Sue.

CHAPTER III

The two Rocking A cowboys dashed out of a little coulee on their horses and galloped them across the sagebrush flat.

The cattle on the flat threw up their tails and scattered in all directions. After Red and Lowly rode through they stopped running, turned their white faces in the same direction, and stared after the cowboys.

Todd laughed. "They all act the same way. They get scared together, then they get curious together."

"Sillies," giggled Sue.

"Red and Lowly are looking for something," said Todd. "Maybe we can help them."

They stood in the Lookout Seat and waved and called. The cowboys turned their horses and galloped to the Rocking A fence. They pulled up below the Lookout Seat.

"Hi, kids!" they called.

"Hi!" Sue and Todd climbed down over the rocks to stand closer to the fence.

"How's everything?" asked Red sociably.

"Fine," said Sue and Todd. No need to bother Red and Lowly with their cow trouble. A cow more or less meant nothing to Red

and Lowly who worked with hundreds of cows.

But today Red and Lowly had cow trouble of their own.

Lowly looked at the fence and began to scold. "There's *another* staple pulled out!"

He took a hammer from his saddle. He dismounted and began to pound a new staple into the nearest fence post to hold up a sagging wire. "A wild maverick's on the loose, trying to tear our fence apart," he said.

Sue and Todd laughed at the frightened way that Lowly rolled his eyes around.

"What's a maverick?" asked Todd, expecting a funny, made-up story.

"A maverick," explained Red, resting his elbow soberly on his saddle horn, "is a range critter without a brand. A heifer, in this case.

She hid from us at roundup time last fall and we didn't get her branded."

"She's locoed, too, if you ask me," said Lowly.

"Locoed?" asked Sue. That word certainly sounded made-up.

But Red explained sensibly, "Sometimes when a range critter eats too much loco weed it begins to act up. This maverick heifer *really* acts up. She spends all her time away from the herd, trying to break through to the other side of our fence."

"It's not natural for a cow to be alone," Lowly said. "It's natural for cows to bunch up. And to stay on their own side of the fence."

"Maybe," said Red thoughtfully, "she is a cow with a plan."

"When she gets big enough," muttered Lowly, "her plan will break a wire and make a hole in the fence. Then she'll let the herd through the hole and it will be *our* plan to find them. If we can."

"Why don't you rope her?" asked Todd.

"Rope her!" snorted Lowly. "We can't even find her. She hides when she sees us."

Red said soberly, "Lowly here is about to offer a big reward for her capture."

"*That's* a joke," laughed Lowly. "Right this minute I wouldn't give two cents for her." He swung into his saddle.

"Well, so long, kids."

"So long."

Red and Lowly rode along the fence, looking for their maverick and for the pulled staples and loose wires she left for them to mend.

Sue and Todd climbed back to the Lookout Seat.

Sue took up the field glasses. "I'm going to try to find the maverick for Red and Lowly."

"I'm all mixed up about that maverick," said Todd. "Let's hunt for her some other time. Today let's pretend that Red and Lowly told us that we could take our pick of any one of their cows. Which one would you pick, Sue?"

CHAPTER IV

Take Your Pick was one of their games.

Sue looked carefully at the Rocking A herd through the field glasses. "I wouldn't know which cow to pick," she said at last. "They're all so much alike."

"Even without the glasses I can see one cow that looks different," said Todd. "I mean that little white-face coming up out of the draw below us. She's walking straight toward the fence. She's hurrying. See her?"

"I see her," said Sue. "It's the maverick heifer, Todd! She has no brand on her left shoulder!" Excitement came into Sue's voice.

Todd took a look. "It's the little maverick, all right! She hid from Red and Lowly in the draw. They're gone now, so she's coming back to the fence to find a place to get through."

"She's down on her knees!" said Sue, looking closely. "She's trying to crawl under the fence!"

"I heard a wire stretch way up here," said Todd. "She's not locoed," he went on, when it was his turn with the glasses. "She's just different from the rest of the herd. *Inside.* She isn't satisfied to live her life on that side of the fence and be like all the others. She wants to get to *our* side—for a reason."

"Was Red joking about her plan?" asked Sue. "Or did Red mean what he said?"

"Sure Red meant it!" All at once Todd was not mixed up about the little maverick. Todd *knew*. "She wants to be a milch cow instead of a beef cow. That's her plan! That's the reason she wants to get away from the others to our side. It *couldn't* be anything else, Sue!"

There was a breathless moment while they thought about that. For a beef cow to want to become a milch cow was a wonderful thing. For her to want to get to *their* side of the fence was a still more wonderful thing.

It looked like a hopeless thing, too.

Sue said, "She is such a little cow. And the

fence is full of barbs. And it is long and strong."

"She is strong, too," said Todd, "because she has a plan. Just think, Sue, she's been here all the time with the other cattle and we never noticed that she is different. Not until today. Not until our cow died."

Just then the little maverick cow saw them far up on the Lookout Seat. She stood very still, looking up at them over the fence.

Sue and Todd sat very quietly, looking down at her over the fence.

Sue said softly, holding the field glasses close, "She has the sweetest face, Todd! I like her. I'll pick her!"

"So will I," said Todd.

The little maverick kicked up her heels. She did a funny little bucking dance on the grass beside the fence. Then she turned and ran out of sight in the draw.

Sue laughed and hugged Todd. "She's showing off because we picked her!"

They climbed down from the Lookout Seat. The game was over for that day.

They had seen the little maverick cow. She was different. So after that everything was different for Sue and Todd, too.

CHAPTER V

They thought about her all the time.

It was not a game any more. It was something real. It was wondering. It was wanting and knowing they couldn't have.

It was a secret, locked in their hearts.

They talked softly about her when they picked corn for the young pigs, and gathered eggs, and washed and wiped dishes, and pulled mustard weeds in the wheat.

They dreamed about her at night.

They looked for her every day from the Lookout Seat.

Now that she had seen them, she looked for them, too. She began to take her nap close to the fence below the Lookout Seat. Sometimes she stopped among the rocks to chew her cud and look up at them out of sober brown eyes. Close up this way, through their glasses, they could see her ears turned like sugar scoops toward them. They could

see the rusty freckles against the white of her cheek, and the curl at the end of her tail as she brought it across her back to switch off flies.

Once, looking straight at them, she lifted her head and lowed. The sound of it hurt their throats the way a bugle call hurts. It was a call to stand together no matter what.

Once she reached fiercely through the fence below the Lookout Seat, making the wires shriek with her weight. It made Sue and Todd hold their breath.

One day they watched her hide from Red and Lowly under a high clump of tumble-weeds that the wind had piled in the fence just below the Lookout Seat. She stood at their feet, looking up at them through the mound of dried weeds. With the field glasses

they could see a deep scratch on the white of her face where a barbed wire had torn her hide. And it tore their hearts.

They watched Red and Lowly search for her. The two cowboys scattered the cattle on the sagebrush flat. They hunted on the west slope, breaking up the line that was going to drink. Finally they gave up. Through the field glasses Sue and Todd watched the cowboys sit on their horses, wiping their foreheads with their red handkerchiefs and scolding to each other.

"I'm not going to tell on her," said Sue.

"She trusts us," said Todd. But he felt uncomfortable as he watched Red and Lowly ride off toward the Rocking A Ranch. "Red and Lowly are our neighbors and best friends," he said.

"And so is the little maverick cow," Sue reminded him.

After a while Sue said, "We must go now, Todd. We promised Mother to help with Jody."

Jody had cried for three days because he didn't like his formula. He began to lose weight. Mother was worried. Jody needed fresh cow's milk long before the wheat crop was in.

CHAPTER VI

One hot day in July, Red and Lowly were out of sorts when they rode up. They dismounted and began to scold about the loose wires and wobbly posts in the fence below the Lookout Seat.

"Don't you ever get sight of our maverick through those glasses of yours?" asked Lowly. "From the sorry looks of this fence she must hang out around here."

Sue said honestly, "We have seen her. Lots of times."

All at once Todd had to know about something. "If she *should* get through the fence—what then?"

"She'd be a stray," said Red. "A lost cow without a brand."

"You'd hunt for her and try to get her back, wouldn't you?" asked Todd.

Lowly jerked at a loose wire. "We wouldn't lift a hand to get her back," he said crossly.

"Lowly isn't as hard-hearted as he sounds," Red explained with a grin to Sue and Todd. "Lowly means that if our maverick once gets through the fence he wouldn't want to spoil her plan by bringing her back. You see, no matter which side of the fence she's on, we're on her side."

Sue and Todd watched with puzzled faces as Red and Lowly rode away.

Todd was more mixed up than ever. He tried to think it out. "They don't want her. She tears down their fence. So if she gets through to our side they wouldn't lift—"

"Let's not get notions," said Sue. "Red and Lowly were hot and tired from mending fence. They didn't mean what they said."

When they got back to the house that afternoon they found Mother rocking Jody. And Mother was singing! Even Jody was singing!

A letter had come from Aunt Matilda. Aunt Matilda lived in a big brick house way back East in the State of Maine. In her letter was a train ticket and two half-fare train tickets.

"July must be hot and dry out there in

Montana," Aunt Matilda wrote Mother. "Why don't you bring the children back to spend the rest of the summer and fall with me? The woods are cool and we have a fresh cow. . . ."

Dad said that Aunt Matilda's invitation was very generous. Mother said that it seemed to solve their problem. Dad planned thoughtfully that he could stay on at Knoll Ranch, alone, and get the wheat crop in. After that he might join them at Aunt Matilda's and—well, they wouldn't decide about anything until next week.

Sue gave Jody a quick hug to let him know that she would be glad for him to have fresh milk from Aunt Matilda's fresh cow back in Maine. Then without saying anything she and Todd went out to water the horses.

Next morning after breakfast Mother planned with Sue and Todd to sort out their toys in the old steamer trunk. "There are lots of them that you don't play with any more."

It wasn't much fun, because emptying a trunk was too much like getting ready for a trip. Slowly Sue and Todd sorted out puzzles with lost pieces and battered dump trucks and dolls with dented cheeks. Their hearts were glad for Jody. But their hearts were heavy, too, because they didn't want to leave Knoll Ranch. If they once left their little wheat ranch anything might happen. They might never come back.

Todd began to talk like Lowly, who didn't always mean what he said. "Anyway, beef cows don't give enough milk to make them worth milking."

Sue talked sensibly, like Sue. "Lowly winked when he said that because cowboys don't like to milk cows. *We* know that the little maverick cow is different from all other beef cows. So her milk would be different. And it would be more."

Todd talked like Todd again. "Lowly knows a lot about cattle, but not everything. If we had her, and she had a calf, and if we fed her our wheat, and kept her in our barn—"

"And loved her," said Sue—

"Then," said Todd, "she would give us lots of milk. Jody would like his bottle again. He would grow fast. Mother would sing *all* the time. We could all stay at Knoll Ranch and be happy together always. And the little maverick cow would be happy, too."

One little maverick cow could make a lot of things right.

Early Sunday morning before the sun was up Sue and Todd got quietly out of bed. They took the field glasses from the hook, saddled Calico, and started up the trail to the Lookout Seat. They had a feeling that it might be their last time. Today was the beginning of the week. Today Mother and Dad would decide about the trip to Aunt Matilda's.

All at once Todd halted Calico. "There she comes, Sue!" he gasped.

Sue looked up. The little maverick cow was coming down the knoll trail to meet them.

She stopped and looked at them. Just then the little plains birds started their early morning song in the grass. The sun came up behind her, making a golden fuzz all around her. She was like something walking out of their dreams.

Sue and Todd scarcely breathed, looking up at this little cow that was different from all others.

At last she had got through to their side of the fence. At last she had accomplished her plan. She waited for them to rein their pony aside, to let her come on down their trail into their empty cow barn and be their milch cow.

There was no one to say that she could not come.

There was no mark on her that said she belonged to anybody. She was a little lost cow that nobody else wanted or loved. A stray. Red and Lowly wouldn't give two cents for her. They wouldn't lift a hand to get her back.

Sue and Todd looked at her with their hearts wide open.

Still, they did not move aside to let her come on.

They knew that it didn't matter what the three of them wanted so much. It didn't matter that she had got through to their side of the fence. It didn't matter whether or not Red and Lowly meant what they said. Only one thing mattered: *She was not their cow.* You do not take something that is not yours. You take some other way to help your Jody, some way that is a right way, even though that way may break your heart.

Sue and Todd started Calico slowly up the knoll trail, making little pushing motions with their hands to drive the little maverick cow back to her own side of the fence.

At first she stood and stared at them.

"She can't believe that we've turned against her," choked Todd.

"She thinks we don't want her," sobbed Sue. "She trusted us, and now we've failed her."

The little maverick cow gave a slow sad shake of her head. Then she turned and went back up the knoll trail toward the Rocking A fence, to find the hole that she had worked so long to make.

CHAPTER VIII

When they reached the top of the knoll, the little maverick cow went straight to the fence. Her white head was low. She made a moaning sound deep in her body.

Suddenly Todd drew rein and looked about him. "The Rocking A herd is gone!" he said in surprise.

It didn't take field glasses to see that there were no more cattle on the sagebrush flat, or on the west slope. The high Montana plains were like a great plate scraped clean. There was nothing left of the herd of beef cattle but a low cloud of dust on the horizon.

"Red and Lowly have driven the herd away!" gasped Sue.

The little maverick cow stopped at the fence, then drew away from it.

"There isn't any hole in the fence," said Todd, puzzled.

They dismounted and walked closer to the fence.

"There *was* a hole here," said Sue. "I can see a new splice in the wire, and some new staples in this post."

"I think I know what happened," said Todd after a moment. "She broke through to our side. Then she saw Red and Lowly coming, so she hid over here. They mended the fence. They didn't know she got through. She *can't* get back to her side now, Sue."

They stood there, thinking.

Just then they saw a piece of paper tacked with a staple to a fence post.

"It's a note," said Sue.

It was from Red and Lowly.

Together they read it.

Dear Kids:

The Rocking A herd is sold and we are going far away. Will you do us a favor? Next time you see our maverick cow will you please take her in and do the best you can by her? We know it is asking a lot of such nice kids as you to be bothered by such a nuisance as this maverick cow, but we are too soft-hearted to leave any critter alone on these plains. It just isn't natural for a cow to be alone. So give her a good home. She'll have a calf soon. Good-bye.

Your friends,

Red and Lowly

P.S. We mean what we say.

P.S.S. We don't know where you'll find her. She's got us so mixed up by now we don't know *which* side of the fence she's on!

Sue and Todd stared at each other when they finished reading the note. Then they began to laugh. They hugged each other. They cried a little, too. They took hands and danced for joy on the grass.

The little maverick cow belonged to them!

There was no more wondering and wanting and knowing they couldn't have.

Red and Lowly had given their maverick cow to them. Red and Lowly meant what they said.

Suddenly Todd stopped dancing and looked around.

"Where has she gone?" he gasped.

The little maverick cow had disappeared!

Then Sue ran to the edge of the knoll where she could see their ranch buildings below. She gave a happy little giggle. "Where *would* you suppose our milch cow would go?"

"To our cow barn, of course!" Todd grinned, hurrying to stand beside her.

Their little maverick cow had wasted no time in rejoicing. She had gone down the knoll trail ahead of them. She must have run. Already they saw that she was across the pasture, hurrying toward the corral gate.

The door to the cow barn was open. From the top of the knoll Sue and Todd watched her walk into the dark emptiness of the barn. She turned around. The next moment her calm white face looked out at them. And their cow barn was empty no more.

Todd sprang to mount Calico. "Hurry, Sue! We've got to get down to the house and tell Mother and Dad to send those train tickets back to Aunt Matilda."

"With love and thanks," added Sue, climbing up behind him with Red and Lowly's note in her hand.

"Sure, with love and thanks," agreed Todd, whose heart was brimming with love and thanks. "We're not leaving Knoll Ranch. *We've got us a cow!*"